# MYSTERY UNDER THE BIG TOP

## by Bonnie West • pictures by Patt Blumer

CAROLRHODA BOOKS
MINNEAPOLIS, MINNESOTA U.S.A.

To the Hardimans

30578

Manufactured in the United States of America

International Standard Book Number: 0-87614-175-0
Library of Congress Catalog Card Number: 81-68852

1   2   3   4   5   6   7   8   9   10   87   86   85   84   83   82

A
CAROLRHODA
MINI-
MYSTERY

"I see great adventure and excitement. I see mystery and intrigue."

"Oh, no!" said Grampa George with a laugh. "That's enough, Freida. Jane and Eddy have plenty of adventure already without any help from you!"

The four of them were sitting in Freida the Fortune Teller's trailer. Jane and Eddy could hardly believe their good luck. All their lives they had heard Grampa George's circus stories. Today they had found out that Grampa George really did know all about the circus. He had introduced Jane and Eddy to most of the performers.

Eddy's favorite was Ian the Incredible. He was the tightrope walker.

"Ian is one of the best in the world," Freida had told them. "It was a real struggle to get him. He's just over from England. A real English gentleman, he is."

Jane's favorite was Cory the Clown. She liked his droopy frown and streams of tears. But after watching him for a while, Jane had noticed that Cory the Clown wasn't just acting. He really did look sad. She had wondered what was wrong.

Now Eddy and Jane were having their fortunes told by Freida. And she was predicting adventure and excitement!

"I'm glad to see things haven't changed around here," said Grampa George.

"Well," said Freida with a sigh. "Things may *look* the same. But there's trouble brewing."

"What do you mean?" asked Grampa George.

"It's Cory," Freida replied. "He's been getting into a lot of trouble lately. He's been playing some pretty bad practical jokes on the performers."

"He's always been a practical joker," said Grampa George. "He's even played a few on me. But he'd never do anything to hurt anyone."

"I know," said Freida. "That's what puzzles me. But all the performers are mad at him. They're sure he's the one playing the jokes."

"Maybe that's why Cory looks so sad," said Jane.

"It is," said Freida. "Tyrone Von Hopster told him that if he played one more joke, he would be fired."

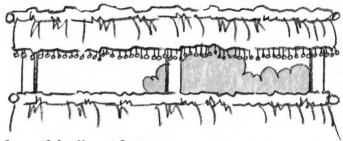

"This is horrible," said Grampa George. "What does Cory say?"

"He says he hasn't played any of the jokes," replied Freida.

"Is there anything we can do to help?" asked Jane.

Suddenly they heard a loud voice. "Hey, you! Stop! Come back here!"

"Uh-oh," said Freida as she jumped up. "That sounds like Tyrone. We'd better go see what's happened."

They found Tyrone standing on the steps of his trailer. There were big spots of paint all over the trailer. And on the door was painted,

Roses are the colour red,
Cotton candy pink.
Everyone who knows you, Tyrone,
Always says you stink.

Tyrone the Ringmaster was furious. He was tapping his toe on the ground. He snapped his whip. His face was bright red.

"Oh, no!" Freida said. "Another joke. Only this is more than a joke. It's vandalism. And Cory *must* have done it."

"Why are you so sure?" asked Eddy.

"Because Cory always talks in rhymes during his act," explained Grampa George. "It's his trademark."

"And if the rhyme isn't enough proof," said Tyrone angrily, "that is!" He pointed to the ground. They could see huge footprints leading away from the trailer.

"Those are Cory's floppy-shoe footprints."

Grampa George had told Jane and Eddy that Cory always wore attachments on his shoes. They made his feet look big and floppy. And there in the dirt were the floppy-shoe footprints.

"And besides," said Tyrone, "I saw someone in floppy shoes racing away just as I opened my door. Someone go and get that fool clown. He's finished in this circus!"

Cory got to Tyrone's trailer a moment later. The other performers were there too.

"Well," snapped Tyrone. "Do you have anything to say for yourself?"

"I didn't do it," replied Cory. "I know that's hard to believe. But I haven't played any of these jokes."

Eddy noticed that Jane was studying the footprints in the dirt. She always seemed to look at things more closely than other people did.

Tyrone was telling Cory to get his things and leave the circus when Jane interrupted.

"Why does everyone think the footprints belong to Cory?" she asked.

"Jane," said Grampa George. "Cory always wears those floppy shoes. You saw them when you watched him practice. He has them on right now for that matter."

"I know," said Jane. "But look at the footprints and then look at Cory's shoes. Those footprints don't match the ones Cory would make. Someone else must have worn the attachments and made those

footprints. Someone *without* heels on their shoes. Cory's shoes have heels. But there aren't any heel marks in the prints around the trailer. So Cory couldn't have made them."

"He could have been wearing different shoes," said Tyrone.

"That's possible," Eddy piped up. "But that would mean that Cory changed his shoes. And you said you saw someone running away when you came out. Cory's trailer is way on the other side of the circus. So he wouldn't have had time to go back to his trailer and change into the shoes he has on now."

"Anyway," said Jane, "there's another reason I'm sure Cory didn't do this."

"What do you mean?" asked Grampa George. Everyone was looking at Jane.

"The answer is in the rhyme on the trailer. I think someone used it to frame Cory. There's a misspelled word in the rhyme. At least to an American it's misspelled. Look at the word color. It's spelled C-O-L-O-U-R. That's not how an American

ROSES ARE THE
COLOUR RED,
COTTON CANDY
PINK
EVERYONE WHO
KNOWS YOU
TYRONE
ALWAYS SAYS

would spell it. But it is the way an English person would spell it. Ian the Incredible must have done all this. He's the only English person in the circus. And he wears slippers instead of shoes, so he would have made footprints like these."

Everyone turned and stared at Ian.

"Yes, you're right. I did it," Ian said suddenly. "I'm sorry. I just wanted to get my twin brother, Rupert, into the circus. He's a clown. He was with a circus that closed down. If he doesn't get another job

soon, he'll lose his visa. And then he'll have to go back to England. I just couldn't stand the thought of Rupe being so far away. So I thought if Cory were fired, Rupert would get the job. And now I've lost my own job as well." Ian looked very sad.

"You should have come to me with your troubles, Ian," said Tyrone. "But I'm glad the whole thing is cleared up. Maybe we can work things out now. Have your brother come and see me. We could probably use another clown. That is, if it's all right with Cory."

Cory smiled and nodded his head.

"And Cory," said Tyrone. "We should never have blamed you just because you've always been our practical joker. We're all sorry."

"That's all right," said Cory. "It's all over now. Shall we shake on it?"

The two men shook. Suddenly a stream of water shot out from the flower on Cory's shirt. It hit Tyrone right in the face. Tyrone wiped off his face and started to laugh.

"Now *that's* the kind of joke only Cory would pull!"